MARIA WENGER

WILSON'S WORLD

WILSON'S WORLD

by Edith Thacher Hurd

Pictures by Clement Hurd

HarperCollins*Publishers*

WILSON'S WORLD

ISBN 06-022749-4
ISBN 06-022750-8 (lib. bdg.)
ISBN 0-06-443359-5 (pbk.)
Library of Congress Catalog Card Number: 73-146002

To Jemima Row, and the children
of the Taft, California, Primary School.
They all helped us to write this book.

Once there was a boy named Wilson.
Wilson liked to paint pictures,
and sometimes he wrote stories
to go with them.

One day Wilson painted a picture
of a big round world.
"THIS IS WILSON'S WORLD,"
he wrote underneath the picture.

THIS IS WILSON'S WORLD

Then Wilson took some blue paint
and painted the sea and the sky.

"Now I'll paint a big bright sun,"
said Wilson.
So Wilson painted a big bright sun
and underneath he wrote:
"This is the sun that warms the world
that makes the green things grow
on Wilson's World."

No sooner had Wilson done that
than green things did begin
to pop up everywhere: green grass,
tall trees, and beautiful flowers
growing all over Wilson's World.

Then Wilson painted an ichthyosaur
and a dinosaur and a caterpillar
and an earthworm and lots of other animals.
Underneath the picture Wilson wrote:

"These are the animals that eat
the green things that grow in the
earth that is warmed by the sun that
shines on the world that Wilson made."

After that Wilson painted monkeys and chimpanzees.

He painted two cave men
and two cave women.

Now Wilson began to paint other people.
He painted people in Africa
and people in China.
He painted people and people and people.
At first his people lived in caves,
then in tents, then in huts and houses,
and then in castles, and finally
in cities.

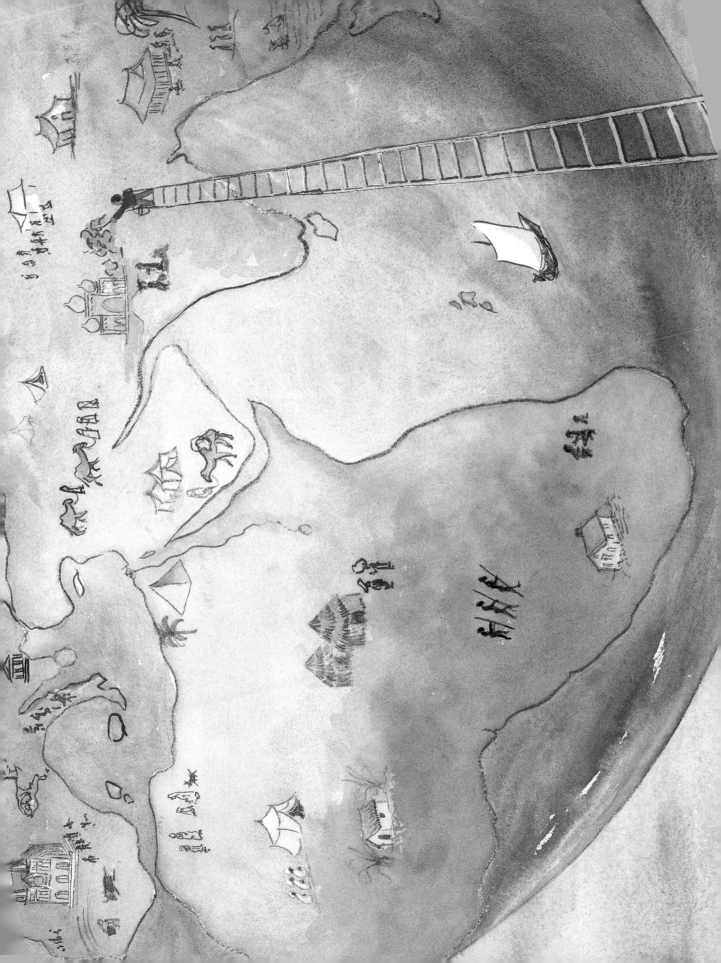

Wilson painted cities and cities
and people and people.
Then Wilson looked at his picture.
"Whew!" said Wilson. "Too many cities
and too many people."

Wilson didn't like all those people
and all of those cities.
So Wilson began to paint a pioneer
going over the mountains and far away.
The pioneer went out to the wide open
prairies where the golden grass grew
and the buffalo roamed.
There were trees to cut,
land to plow and to plant,
and plenty of fish in the rivers
that ran clear and clean to the sea.

Then Wilson painted another pioneer,
just to keep the first one company,
then another and another.
And all of a sudden Wilson found out
that the prairies were beginning
to fill up with people.
There were houses and houses and houses
and pretty soon the houses made towns,
and roads ran all over the prairies
going from town to town.
There were roads for horses,
then wagons, then cars, and at last
motorcycles were pop-pop-popping everywhere.

All the cities and all of the cars

made so much smoke and so much smog

that Wilson couldn't even paint

the blue sky blue, and the yellow sun

could hardly shine down on the cities

or even on the prairies anymore.

"Oh, no!" said Wilson.

"This isn't the kind of world I want.

This isn't MY WORLD!"

So underneath this picture Wilson wrote:

"PHOOEY!"

What could Wilson do now?
He thought and thought.
"What kind of a world do I really want?"

At last, Wilson took
a brand-new piece of paper,
and he painted and painted.
He painted a brand-new world,
with brand-new people
and a brand-new bright-yellow sun,
and all the sky was blue again.

Then Wilson looked to see
what everyone was doing.

"Wow!" said Wilson. "No wonder
all the sky is blue again.
They're not building too many houses
or too many cities. They're not
cutting more trees, or shooting
more buffalo, or catching more of
my fish than they really need.
Everybody cares about my world again."

"They like my rivers clear and clean
so everyone can swim again.

Wow," said Wilson,
"what a beautiful world!"

So right across this picture,
Wilson wrote:

WILSON'S WORLD

Then he put away his paints
and went swimming!